Time to Shine

Read more
Fairylight Friends!

Fairylight Friends
Time to Shine

written by
Jessica Young

illustrated by
Marie Vanderbemden

ACORN™
SCHOLASTIC INC.

For Katie, a fairy great editor—JY

For my mom, who taught me everything except how to write dedication lines —MV

Text copyright © 2021 by Jessica Young

Illustrations copyright © 2021 by Marie Vanderbemden

Library of Congress Cataloging-in-Publication Data

Names: Young, Jessica (Jessica E.), author. | Vanderbemden, Marie, illustrator.
Title: Time to shine / written by Jessica Young ; illustrated by Marie Vanderbemden.
Description: First edition. | New York : Acorn/Scholastic Inc., 2020. |
Series: Fairylight friends ; 2
Summary: Winter has come to the Fairy Forest, and best friends
Ruby, Iris, and Pip are eager to sample all the winter activities
available like making snow fairies, sledding, and brewing snowflake
tea—and building a simple greenhouse so Pip can start his garden despite the snow.
Identifiers: LCCN 2019058991 (print) | ISBN 9781338596557 (paperback) |
ISBN 9781338596564 (library binding) | ISBN 9781338596571 (ebook)
Subjects: LCSH: Fairies—Juvenile fiction. | Winter—Juvenile fiction. |
Snow—Juvenile fiction. | Best friends—Juvenile fiction. |
CYAC: Fairies—Fiction. | Winter—Fiction. | Snow—Fiction. |
Best friends—Fiction. | Friendship—Fiction.
Classification: LCC PZ7.Y8657 Ti 2020 | DDC 813.6 [E]—dc23
LC record available at https://lccn.loc.gov/2019058991

10 9 8 7 6 5 4 3 2   21 22 23 24 25

Printed in China   62
First edition, January 2021

Edited by Katie Carella
Book design by Maria Mercado

Table of Contents

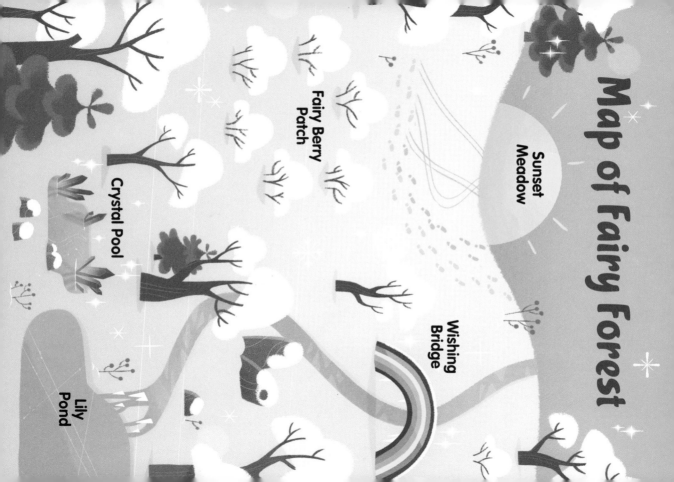

Map of Fairy Forest

Sunset Meadow

Fairy Berry Patch

Crystal Pool

Wishing Bridge

Lily Pond

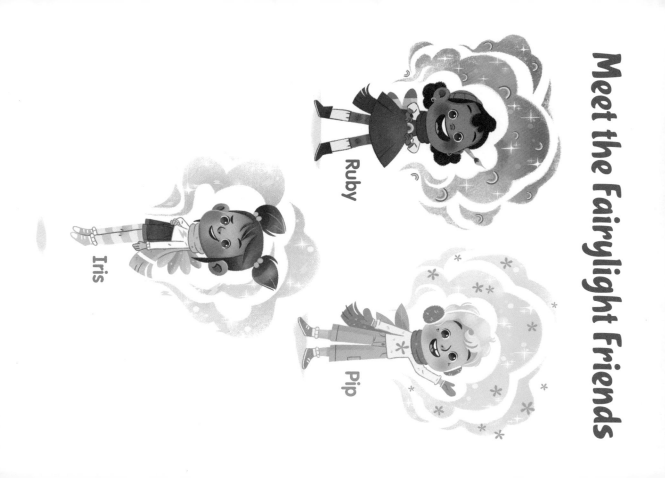

Meet the Fairylight Friends

Ruby

Iris

Pip

Snowflake Tea

Iris woke up early.

It's a snowy day!

She raced to find
her friends.

Ruby was ready.

Let's play!

Pip was sleeping.

Wake up, Pip!

The friends made tracks in the snow.

CRUNCH!

CRUNCH!

CRUNCH!

They made snow fairies.

SWISH!

SWISH!

SWISH!

Then they caught sparkly snowflakes in a jar.

Gotcha!

ZOOM!

Ruby, Iris, and Pip flew to school to show their teacher.

Hi, Miss Goldwing!

Iris pulled out the jar.

Your snowflakes got warm and melted.

Ohh.

But you can make snowflakes that won't melt!

Miss Goldwing passed out paper.

The friends drew snowflakes.

Then Ruby had an idea! She grabbed the jar. She poured the snowflake water into a teapot.

There was a puff of pink fairy dust!

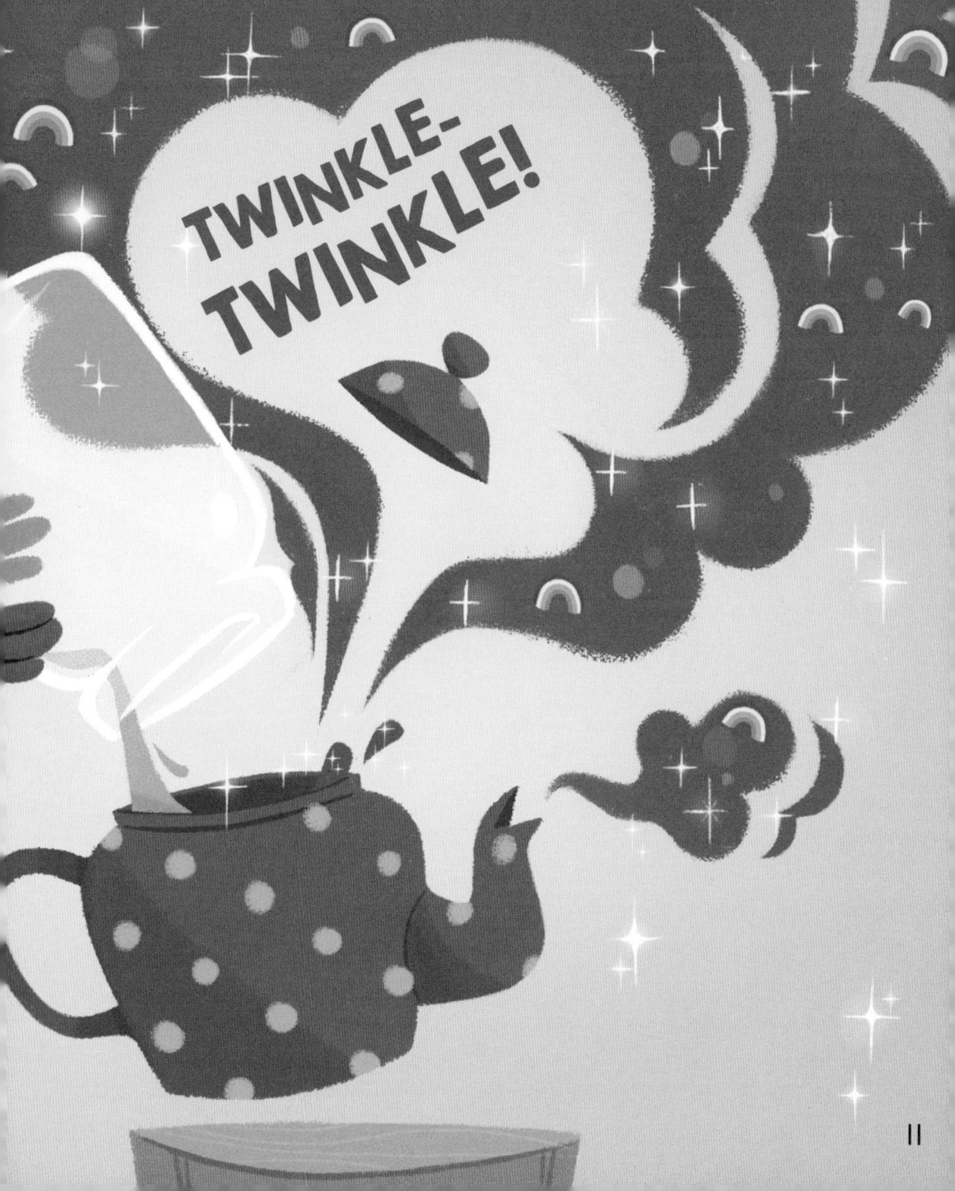

Winter Warmers

It was the coldest day of winter.
Iris and Pip were at Ruby's house.

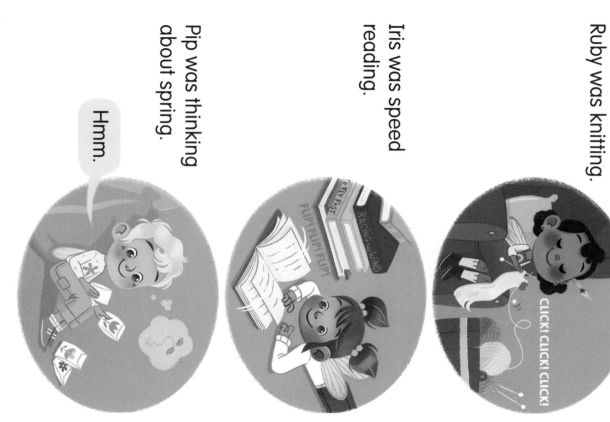

Ruby was knitting.

Iris was speed reading.

Pip was thinking about spring.

Hmm.

Iris looked out the window.

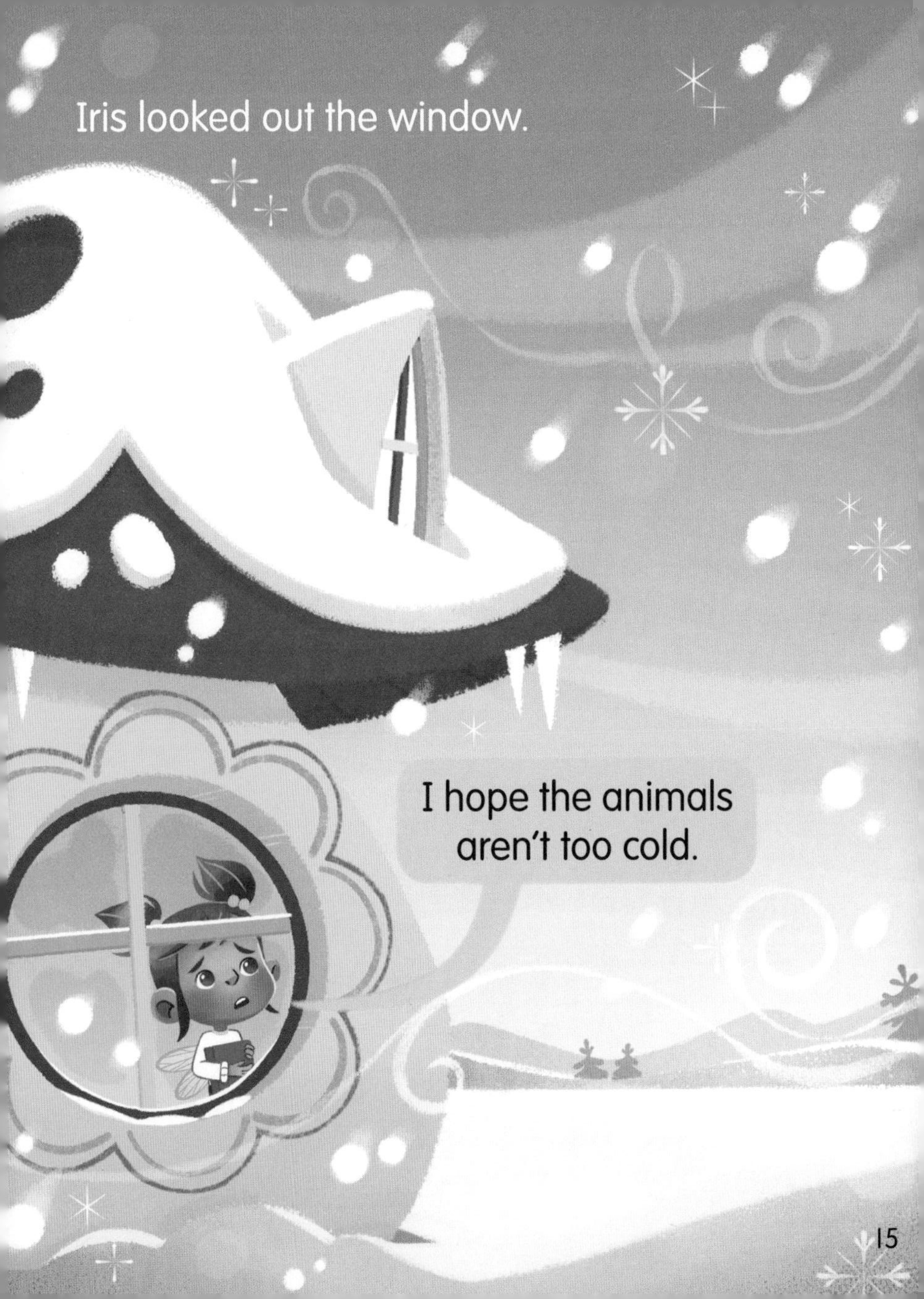

Ruby held up her knitting.

We can knit things to help them stay warm!

I don't know how to knit.

I don't either.

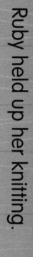

Ruby showed Iris and Pip how to knit.

Ruby knit hats and mittens.

Pip knit scarves and blankets.

Iris knit all kinds of things.

CLICK! CLICK! CLICK! CLICK! CLICKETY!
CLICKETY! CLICK! CLICK!

Look what I made!

We are great knitters!
The animals will be so warm!

These wing warmers will keep **us** warm too.

Ooh! Thanks!

The friends were ready to take the animals their gifts. Iris opened the door.

Hello, snow!

Whoa!

C-c-cold!

Ruby and Iris wrapped Pip up.

They carried him to the sled.

ZOOOOOM!

Then Iris took off in a puff of blue fairy dust.

A Place to Grow

Ruby and Iris knocked on Pip's door.

Pip looked sad.

Hi, Pip! What's wrong?

I miss my garden. I wish spring would come.

Ruby, Iris, and Pip collected branches.

Yippeeee!

The friends worked hard.

Then Ruby added her magic touch.

Twinkle time!

TWINKLE!
TWINKLE!

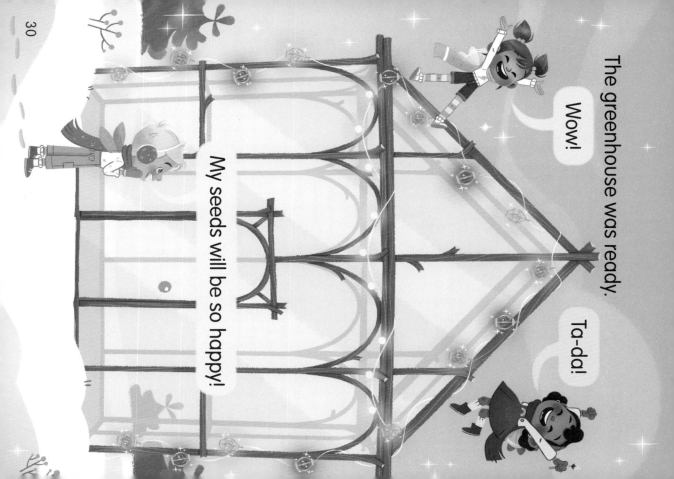

Pip planted
his seeds.

Iris watered
them.

The sun warmed
them.

Then Pip showered the seeds with magic.

Ready, set — grow!

Pip's new garden grew.

The Sniffles

Ruby, Iris, and Pip were ready to sled.

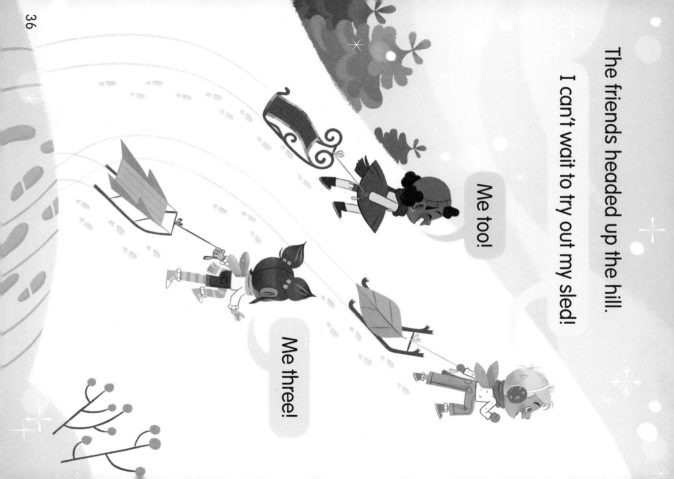

They pulled their sleds to the top.

Ruby slid down.

WHEEEEE!

Pip slid down.

WOO-HOOOOOO!

Iris stopped to rest.

Whew.

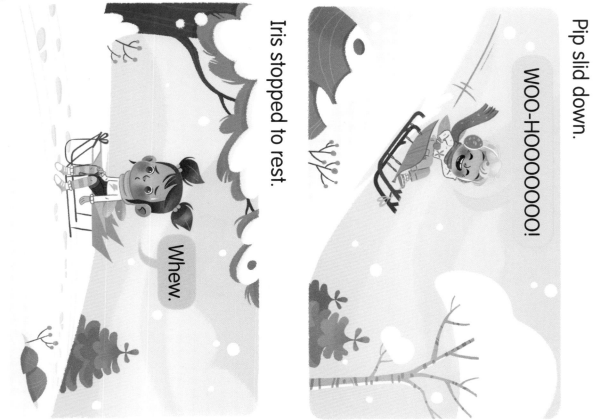

Ruby and Pip came back.

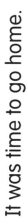

It was time to go home.

Let's go.

Ruby and Pip gave Iris a ride.

Ruby took her some soup.

Pip took her some flowers.

Iris had a long sleep.

The next day, Ruby and Pip went to see Iris.

Hi, Iris!

How are you feeling?

Ready to sled!

Snowstorm

Ruby, Iris, and Pip flew to school in a snowstorm. The wind howled. The snow swirled.

The classroom was quiet.

Ruby, Iris, and Pip flew to the top of the school. Ruby made it sparkle.

Time to shine!

TWINKLE - TWINKLE!

Pip made it grow.

Iris added some fairy fireworks.

The school shone like a lighthouse.
Soon the friends spotted their teacher.

MISS GOLDWING!!!

You're here!

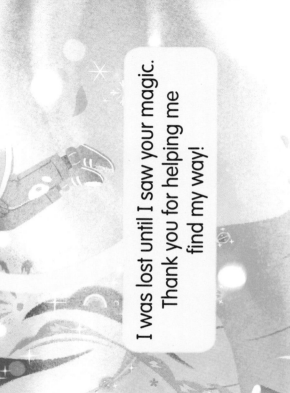

I was lost until I saw your magic. Thank you for helping me find my way!

Ruby, Iris, and Pip took Miss Goldwing inside to warm up.

This is the perfect way to spend a snowy day.

A cozy fire.

Good friends.

And a good book!

About the Creators

JESSICA YOUNG grew up in Ontario, Canada. When she's not making up stories, she loves making art with kids. Her other books include

the Haggis and Tank Unleashed early chapter book series, the Finley Flowers series, *Play This Book, Pet This Book, A Wish Is a Seed,* and *My Blue Is Happy.*

MARIE VANDERBEMDEN works from her barge moored in Belgium. Telling stories through drawing has always been her passion. Marie has worked mainly in the illustration of children's books and animated

movies. Fairylight Friends is the first early reader series she has illustrated. When she is not sketching, she also enjoys photography, sculpture, and teaching ceramics.

YOU CAN DRAW IRIS!

1. Draw four shapes for Iris's head, neck, shirt, and shorts.

2. Add two ears, pigtails, and legs.

3. Draw Iris's arms and the rest of her hair.

4. Draw one lightning bolt, two shoes, and two wings.

5. Add Iris's face, hair ties, knees, and legging details.

6. Color in your drawing!

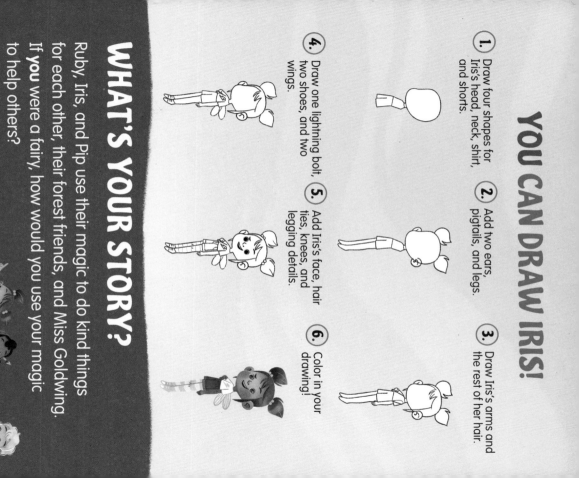

WHAT'S YOUR STORY?

Ruby, Iris, and Pip use their magic to do kind things for each other, their forest friends, and Miss Goldwing.

If **you** were a fairy, how would you use your magic to help others?

Write and draw your story!

scholastic.com/acorn